THE
MAGIC POCKET

SELECTED POEMS

by MICHIO MADO

decorations by MITSUMASA ANNO

translated by THE EMPRESS MICHIKO OF JAPAN

MARGARET K. McELDERRY BOOKS

Also by Michio Mado and illustrated by Mitsumasa Anno

The Animals: Selected Poems

(MARGARET K. McELDERRY BOOKS)

Margaret K. McElderry Books
An imprint of Simon & Schuster Children's Publishing Division
1230 Avenue of the Americas
New York, New York 10020

The English text of this book is set in Usherwood Medium.
The decorations are rendered in hand-painted paper collage.

First Edition

Printed in the United States
10 9 8 7 6 5 4 3 2 1

Library of Congress Catalog Card Number: 97-75774
ISBN 0-689-82137-9

も く じ   CONTENTS

うさぎ

うさぎに　うまれて
うれしい　うさぎ
はねても
はねても
はねても
はねても
うさぎで　なくなりゃしない

うさぎに　うまれて
うれしい　うさぎ
とんでも
とんでも
とんでも
とんでも
くさはら　なくなりゃしない

RABBIT

Being a rabbit,
I'm so happy,
Jumping
Jumping
Jumping
Jumping.
See, I'm a rabbit—nothing else!

Being a rabbit,
I'm so happy,
Hopping
Hopping
Hopping
Hopping.
See, my field has no end.

ひよこちゃんの　やまのぼり

ひよこちゃんが
ふたりで　やまのぼり
おやまは　どこよ
　おかあさんの　せなか
　おかあさんの　せなか

ひよこちゃんが
ふたりで　やまのぼり
おべんとう　なあに
　おこめの　つぶよ
　ひとつぶ　ずつよ

ひよこちゃんが
ふたりで　おやくそく
おやくそく　なあに
　また　こんど　のぼろ
　また　こんど　のぼろ

CHICKS CLIMBING UP A HILL

Two little chickens
Climbed up a hill.
Where's the hill?
"There! Mommy's back,
Mommy's the hill."

Two little chickens
Climbed up a hill.
What's your lunch?
"Grains of rice,
One for each."

Two little chickens
Made a promise.
What was the promise?
"Let's climb again!
Let's climb again!"

ゆび

ゆび
ゆび
ゆび
ならんでるよ
なかよしね

つめ
つめ
つめ
ゆびの　かおよ
かわいいね

FINGERS

Fingers
Fingers
Fingers,
All in a row.
No quarrels.

Nails
Nails
Nails,
Fingers' faces.
Sweet!

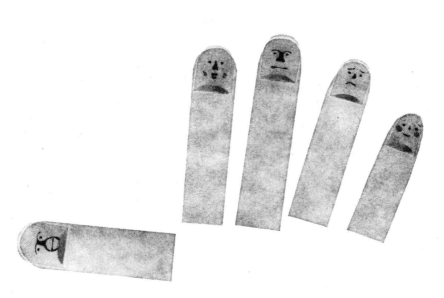

あそびましょ

あそびましょって
ぞうさんが
わたしの　いえに
きたら　いい
ね　そうですね
おかあさん

あそびましょって
くまさんも
わたしの　いえに
きたら　いい
ね　そうですね
おかあさん

LET'S PLAY TOGETHER

Wouldn't it be nice
If a baby elephant
Came to my house,
Saying, "Let's play together."
Wouldn't it be nice,
Mommy?

Wouldn't it be nice
If a baby bear
Came to my house,
Saying, "Let's play together."
Wouldn't it be nice,
Mommy?

ふしぎな　ポケット

ポケットの　なかには
ビスケットが　ひとつ
ポケットを　たたくと
ビスケットは　ふたつ

もひとつ　たたくと
ビスケットは　みっつ
たたいて　みるたび
ビスケットは　ふえる

そんな　ふしぎな
ポケットが　ほしい
そんな　ふしぎな
ポケットが　ほしい

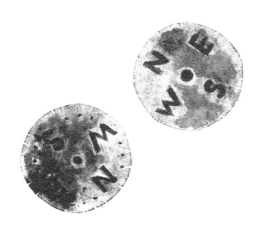

THE MAGIC POCKET

Inside the pocket
There's one cookie.
Hit the pocket,
There are two!

Hit it again,
There are three.
The more I hit it,
The more there are!

I wish I had
A pocket like that!
I wish I had
A pocket like that!

かさの　うた

かさ　かさ
せかいで　いちばん
のんきな　はな
すぼんだり　ひらいたり
あるいたり　はしったり

かさ　かさ
せかいで　いちばん
おおきな　はな
おかあさんも　すっぽりこ
おとうさんも　すっぽりこ

かさ　かさ
せかいで　いちばん
おしゃべりの　はな
あられと　ぺらぺらぺら
あめとも　べらべらべら

SONG OF AN UMBRELLA

Umbrella, umbrella,
The world's
Most happy-go-lucky flower,
Shutting, opening,
Walking, running.

Umbrella, umbrella,
The world's
Biggest flower,
Perfectly covering Mommy,
Perfectly covering Daddy.

Umbrella, umbrella,
The world's
Most chattering flower,
Chattering now with hail,
Chattering now with rain.

あられ

あら
あら
あられ
おでこに　おちた
　ごめんなさいって
　いったかな
　ちいさい　こえで
　いったでしょ

あら
あら
あられ
みてたら　きえた
　さようならって
　いったかな
　ちいさい　こえで
　いったでしょ

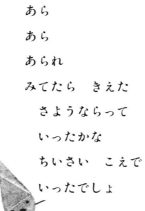

HAIL

Hi
Ho
Hail!
It hit my forehead.
    Did it say, "Sorry"?
    I think it said, "Sorry,"
    But in a tiny, little voice.

Hi
Ho
Hail!
It vanished while I watched.
    Did it say, "Good-bye"?
    I think it said, "Good-bye,"
    But in a tiny, little voice.

やぎさん　ゆうびん

しろやぎさんから　おてがみ　ついた
くろやぎさんたら　よまずに　たべた
しかたがないので　おてがみ　かいた
―さっきの　おてがみ
　　ごようじ　なあに

くろやぎさんから　おてがみ　ついた
しろやぎさんたら　よまずに　たべた
しかたがないので　おてがみ　かいた
―さっきの　おてがみ
　　ごようじ　なあに

THE GOATS AND THE LETTERS

Black Goat received White Goat's letter.
He ate it up before he read it.
"Oo-la-la! What shall I do?"
He wrote a letter asking:
"What, by the way, did your letter say?"

White Goat received Black Goat's letter.
He ate it up before he read it.
"Oo-la-la! What shall I do?"
He wrote a letter asking:
"What, by the way, did your letter say?"

やどかりさん

まいにち　ひっこし
やどかりさん
きょうは　どちら
　ざんぶりなみの
　いっちょうめ
　さんばんち

まいにち　ひっこし
やどかりさん
きょうは　どちら
　でこぼこいわの
　さんちょうめ
　いちばんち

まいにち　ひっこし
やどかりさん
きょうは　どちら
　なんとかやらの
　なんちょうめ
　わすれたよ

HERMIT CRAB

Hermit Crab,
Every day you move.
Where's your house today?
   My new address is:
   Number 1-3
   Under a splash of wave.

Hermit Crab,
Every day you move.
Where's your house today?
   My new address is:
   Number 3-1
   On a rocky rock.

Hermit Crab,
Every day you move.
Where's your house today?
   My new address is:
   Number . . . uh . . . some such street–
   Oh, I forget!

ジャングルジムの　うた

よじって　のぼれ
くぐって　のぼれ
のぼれ　のぼれ
ジャングル　グルグル　ジム
　のぼり　つめたら　てっぺんで
　やっほー　やっほほー
　つめたい　そらに
　ほっぺた　つけろ

よじって　あそべ
くぐって　あそべ
あそべ　あそべ
ジャングル　グルグル　ジム
　あそびあきたら　てっぺんで
　やっほー　やっほほー
　ながれる　くもの
　わたがし　なめろ

22

JUNGLE GYM SONG

Twist and climb,
Crawl through and climb,
Climb up, climb up
the jungle, jungle gym.
    When you reach the goal, there at the top,
    Ya Hô, Ya Ho Hô!
    Touch with your cheeks
    The chilly sky above.

Twist and play,
Crawl through and play,
Play on, play on
the jungle, jungle gym.
    When you are tired of playing, there at the top,
    Ya Hô, Ya Ho Hô!
    Lick the cotton candy
    Of fleecy clouds.

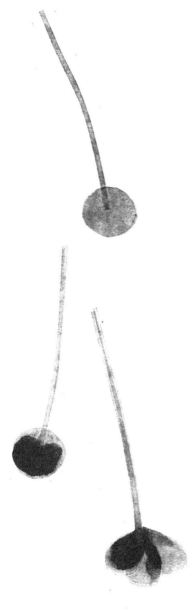

音

ピアノの音　ぽろん
サクランボ　ひとつ

たいこの音　どどん
大波　ひとつ

カスタネット　けけ
おこうこ　ひときれ

らっぱの音　ぺぽー
あんぱん　ひとつ

トライアングル　つーん
かみの毛　一本

すずの音　ちりん
マメの花　ひとつ

もくぎょの音　ぽこん
たんこぶ　ひとつ

うそっこ　うた　たらりー
にじの橋　ひとつ

24

SOUNDS

Sound of a piano–Po Ron,
One plump cherry.

A big bass drum–Do Don,
An enormous wave.

Castanets–Kéké,
A slice of pickle.

Sound of a trumpet–PéPô,
Bread with sweet soybeans.

Triangle–Ti ~ ng
A thread of hair.

Sound of a bell–Chi Rin,
A bean flower.

Sound of a wooden drum–Po Kon,
A bump on the head.

A nonsense song–Ta Ra Ree,
A rainbow bridge!

うさぎさんが　きてね

うさぎさんが　きてね
おなまえ　つけてと
いいました
ピョンタちゃんと　つけたら
ピョンと　はねて
うふんと　わらって　いきました

すずめさんが　きてね
おなまえ　つけてと
いいました
チュンコちゃんと　つけたら
チュンと　ないて
うふんと　わらって　いきました

A RABBIT CAME TO ME

A rabbit came to me
And said, "Please
Give me a name."
When I named him Hoppitty,
He tried a big hop,
Then laughed a little and went away.

A sparrow came to me
And said, "Please
Give me a name."
When I named him Chirpy,
He tried a big chirp,
Then laughed a little and went away.

どんぐりの　うた

どんぐり　どんぐり
こんにちは
あそびなさい
あそびなさい
おてての　おにわで

どんぐり　どんぐり
さようなら
ねむりなさい
ねむりなさい
ポケットの　おうちで

28

SONG TO THE ACORN

Acorn, acorn,
How do you do?
Play around,
Play around,
My hand is your playground.

Acorn, acorn,
I'll see you again.
Sleep well,
Sleep well,
My pocket is your home.

おはよう　おやすみ

おはよう　おはよう
よが　あけた
おとうさんが　おきた
おかあさんが　おきた
おにいさんが　おきた
おねえさんが　おきた
あかちゃんが　おきた
みんなみんな　おきた
おひさま　おはよう

おやすみ　おやすみ
ひが　くれた
あかちゃんが　ねたよ
おねえさんが　ねたよ
おにいさんが　ねたよ
おかあさんが　ねたよ
おとうさんが　ねたよ
みんなみんな　ねたよ
おつきさま　おやすみ

GOOD MORNING AND GOOD NIGHT

Good morning, good morning!
The day breaks.
Daddy's up,
Mommy's up,
Brother's up,
Sister's up,
Baby's up.
Everyone's up.
Good morning, Sun!

Good night, good night!
The day is over.
Baby's in bed,
Sister's in bed,
Brother's in bed,
Mommy's in bed,
Daddy's in bed.
Everyone's in bed.
Good night, Moon!